KU-743-090

Michael Coleman
Illustrated by Nick Abadzis

ORCHARD BOOKS

ORCHARD BOOKS
96 Leonard Street, London EC2A 4XD
Orchard Books Australia
14 Mars Road, Lane Cove, NSW 2066
First published in Great Britain in 2000
First paperback edition 2000
Text © Michael Coleman, 2000
Illustrations © Nick Abadzis, 2000
Cover photograph © Professional Sport
The rights of Michael Coleman to be identified as the author
and Nick Abadzis as the illustrator of this work
have been asserted by them in accordance with the
Copyright, Designs and Patents Act, 1988.
A CIP catalogue record for this book is available
from the British Library.
ISBN 1 86039 935 5 (hbk)
ISBN 1 86039 936 3 (pbk)
1 3 5 7 9 10 8 6 4 2 (hbk)
1 3 5 7 9 10 8 6 4 2 (pbk)
Printed in Great Britain

Contents

1. Superior Skill   6

2. I'll Knock Your Block Off!   17

3. Injury Time   29

4. You Twister!   39

5. The Gambler's Last Throw   48

Coach

Midfield
(Centre)

Left Full
Back

Right Full
Back

Centre
Back

Striker

Goalkeeper

Kirsten
Browne

Barry 'Bazza'
Watts

Daisy
Higgins

Colin 'Colly'
Flower

Tarlock
Bhasin

Lennie
Gould
(captain)

Trev the
Rev

Substitute

Midfield
(Centre)

Centre
Back

Midfield
(Right)

Striker

Midfield
(Left)

Substitute

Mick
Ryall

Jonjo
Rix

Lulu
Squibb

Jeremy
Emery

Rhoda
O'Neill

Lionel
Murgatroyd

Ricky
King

1

Superior Skill

"Leave him to me, guys!"

Bazza Watts, the Angels left-back, jogged confidently out towards the wiry boy dribbling the ball his way. Angels FC were playing a team named Maddox Rebels and the boy with the ball was the Rebels star winger Dylan Thompson, otherwise known as Twister Thompson because he usually had the defender marking him tied up in knots.

But not today. The Angels were 3–0 ahead and Bazza was having a great game. What's more, he was making sure that everyone knew it – especially his opponent.

"Come on, Twister, let's see if you can do better this time," he yelled at Thompson as the winger dribbled nearer. "Twentieth time lucky!"

Bringing the ball close, Twister ducked low and feinted to go to Bazza's right. But Bazza wasn't fooled. He'd seen every one of Twister's tricks so often in the school playground that he knew exactly what was coming next. And so, waiting until the Rebels winger made his move and tried to dribble past, Bazza hit him with a crunching tackle that sent both the ball and player flying into touch.

"So that's why they call you 'Twister'," laughed Bazza. "'Cos you're so good at somersaults!"

Glaring angrily, Thompson picked himself up. "Gimme the ball!" he screeched to his team-mate taking the throw-in. "His luck can't last!"

Bazza laughed again. "Luck? It's not luck, Twister. It's skill. Superior skill."

Bringing the ball under control, Thompson dribbled forward again. Ahead of him, Bazza yawned. "Come on then. Bet you five pounds you can't get past me."

"Five pounds?"

"Five lovely pounds," repeated Bazza, grinning. "But try something different this time, eh? The bet's off if I get so bored I fall asleep."

"Right!" snarled Thompson. "You're on. Say goodbye to your money, Wattso!"

Gritting his teeth with determination, Twister stepped his left foot over the ball in an attempt to send Bazza the wrong way. The Angels full-back didn't move.

"Bo-ring," sighed Bazza.

Thompson tried again. He twisted to his right. Bazza went with him. He dummied to sprint forward. Bazza didn't move. He darted forward. Bazza was in position at once, blocking his way.

"Give in, yet?" laughed Bazza.

Desperately, Thompson tried the only trick he hadn't tried – putting his foot under the ball to scoop it up into the air and over Bazza's head.

The Angels defender saw it coming. The instant Twister's foot went under the ball, Bazza sailed in with a tackle like a sledge-hammer – and Thompson sailed into the air again, to turn another perfect somersault!

"You want to take up high-diving, Twister! You'd get full marks every time!"

Thompson scowled at the Angels full-back. "You're going to pay for this, Wattso."

"Wrong, Twister," laughed Bazza as the referee's whistle shrieked, "You're the one who's going to be doing the paying. That's full-time, and you didn't get past me – so I win the bet!"

"You don't mean it? I haven't got five pounds!"

"Sorry, Twister, a bet's a bet. Tell you what, I'll give you a couple of days to raise the money. You can give it to me Wednesday. A nice crisp five pound note will do nicely!"

"You had a good game Bazza," said Tarlock Bhasin in the changing rooms afterwards.

"Good?" snorted Bazza. "I wasn't good, Tarlock, I was brilliant! Twister didn't get past me once."

"Only because he couldn't get round your big head without taking the ball out of play," said Lulu Squibb.

"Out of the country, you mean," laughed Colly Flower.

"You're just jealous, Lulu," said Bazza. "Jealous of my superior skill."

Lulu's eyes flashed. "Superior skill? You big banana, I've got more skill in my pigtails than you've got in your whole body! I'll beat you at anything!"

"You want to bet?"

"Yeah!" shouted Lulu. "Name it!"

But before Bazza could do just that,
the argument was interrupted by Trev, the
Angels coach, calling them to attention.

"Training on Tuesday!" he called. "And
I'll be trying something new."

"What's that, Trev?" asked Lennie
Gould, excitedly.

In real life their coach was the vicar of
St Jude's Church, but it had always been
said that he'd been a good enough
footballer to turn professional if he hadn't
wanted to be a vicar more. So when Trev
talked football they all listened.

"Throw-ins," said Trev.

"Throw-ins?" echoed Mick Ryall, disappointed. "Great. Not."

"*Long* throw-ins," said Trev, emphasising the 'long'. "We're playing Welby Wolves next week and they're not so hot at defending crosses from the right. So I want to surprise them by aiming some long throw-ins at them as well – which means finding out who's got the longest throw."

The moment Trev left the room, Bazza turned back to Lulu. "So you can beat me at anything, can you?"

"Anything!" snapped Lulu, jutting out her chin defiantly. "You name it, Bragger Watts, and I can beat you at it!"

"In that case, I bet you…"

"Bet me?" gulped Lulu.

Bazza nodded, smiling. Offering to bet Twister Thompson out on the pitch had been a bit of an accident, the words slipping out in the heat of the moment. But having won that bet, Bazza found himself simply unable to resist trying to win another one – especially when the idea he'd just had was a sure-fire certainty.

"Yes, I bet you…five pounds! That my throw-in will be longer than your throw-in."

Lulu snorted. "So that's what you want to bet, is it?"

She moved threateningly close to Bazza, jabbing her finger at his chest.

"Well let me tell you, Bazza the Bighead…" Jab. "Nothing would give me greater pleasure than to take your money…" Jab. "So the answer is…"

"Yes?" said Bazza eagerly.

"Er...no," replied Lulu. She turned away.

"No?" sneered Bazza. "No? Why not?"

"Because a chimpanzee like you could beat me at throw-ins with one hand tied behind your back," snapped Lulu. "You know it – and so do I!"

2

I'll Knock Your Block Off!

Bazza walked home lost in thought. What a pity Lulu hadn't let her temper get the better of her and accepted his challenge. The prospect of another winning bet had really excited him – and still did.

He was certain he could produce a longer throw-in than Lulu. He was a big and muscular boy. She was a titchy, weedy girl with a fire-cracker for a brain. Of course he could beat her. Even she thought he could. What had she said? *"You could beat me at throw-ins with one hand tied behind your back."*

A slow smile crossed Bazza's face. One hand tied behind his back? Yes, that was how to do it...

Lulu was already on her way out of the changing room when Bazza turned up for the practice session on Tuesday night. When she saw the Angels defender, she stopped dead.

"What have you done to yourself?" she gasped.

Bazza's wrist was bandaged and his arm nestled in a huge white sling. "I don't want to talk about it," he groaned.

"Good job I didn't bet you about the throw-in competition then, wasn't it?" said Lulu.

"Why?" replied Bazza, looking as though he didn't understand.

"Because with a bad wrist, you don't stand a chance of beating me. So if that bet was on, I'd be about to take your money."

Bazza snorted. "You? Take my money? You must be joking! I could have one arm in plaster and the other held on by sticky tape and I'd still be able to take a longer throw-in than you!"

"Oh you would, would you?" retorted Lulu, her pigtails swinging threateningly.

"Easy-squeezy, double-sneezy," said Bazza. "I'm still prepared to bet you."

"Oh you are, are you?" yelled Lulu, almost bursting with rage. "Right, a bet it is! Get ready to kiss your five pounds goodbye!"

Trev got the competition under way right at the start of the session. Lining the squad up along the right touchline, he drew lots for the order they'd take their throws. Lulu's name came out of the hat last, with Bazza's immediately before hers.

"You'll know you can't win before you even pick up the ball," hissed Bazza.

"I'll know I've got nothing to beat, you mean," snapped Lulu.

Each of the squad took three throw-ins, aiming the ball as far as they could into the goal mouth. In each case, Trev stuck a small marker into the ground to show where their best throw had landed.

As his turn drew near, Bazza had a good look at what he had to beat. The nearest marker belonged to Lionel Murgatroyd. He'd been credited with a one-metre throw for trying after the ball had slipped out of his hands and actually ended up behind him!

The markers for Jonjo Rix, Rhoda O'Neill, Tarlock Bhasin and Daisy Higgins were all pretty level, each of them having managed to get their throws as far as the edge of the penalty area.

A metre or so further away were the markers for Colly Flower, Mick Ryall and Jeremy Emery, with those for Kirsten Browne and Lennie Gould another metre beyond them.

Ahead of them all, though, was Ricky King's. After an opening foul, when he'd forgotten he couldn't use just one hand as he used to when he was playing American Football[1] and had launched the ball on to the roof of the changing room, he'd managed to get a legal throw-in almost as far as the edge of the six-yard box.

[1] See *Handball Horror!*

"Good one, Ricky," called Trev. "Your turn, Bazza. Do your best."

"Not that it'll be good enough," said Lulu.

"No?" smirked Bazza. "I bet it will be good enough. Especially when—"

Shrugging his arm out of its sling, Bazza whirled it cheerfully round and round like a high-speed windmill.

"Wha– wha–" gurgled Lulu as she realised she'd been tricked. "You cheating stinker! You said you'd hurt your arm!"

"No I didn't," said Bazza innocently. "You asked me what I'd done to myself,

23

and I said I didn't want to talk about it. And I didn't!"

"But – but – the bet..."

"Is on!" cried Bazza. "Watch this for a throw-in, Lulu!"

Picking up the ball, Bazza took a few steps back from the touchline and ran in for his first throw. It was a corker. Sailing out of his hands it flew past Ricky's marker to land almost level with the near goalpost!

"I think that should be good enough," he smirked. "I won't bother about my other two throws. Your go, Lulu."

And with that he swaggered off across to where Trev was placing his marker. By the time he got there, Lulu was winding up for her first throw. With a huff and a puff she ran in and heaved the ball a good five metres short of Bazza's mark.

"Not a bad try," called Bazza, before adding, "a terrible one!"

Snatching up another ball, Lulu steamed up for her second throw. In spite of all her effort it got no further than the first one.

"Hopeless!" hooted Bazza. "Call that a throw-in? Lulu Squibb, you couldn't throw a party!"

Doubling up with laughter, he hardly noticed as the seething Lulu grabbed her third ball and stomped backwards for her longest run-up yet. He only realised that she was about to take her final throw when she roared up to the touchline like a steam train, stopped, whirled her arms over in a blur and, with a window-rattling cry of "Yaaaaaahhhhhh!!!" launched the ball straight at his head!

Bazza didn't have a moment to lose. As the ball zoomed towards him like a shot fired from a cannon, he dived out of the way.

"Missed me!" he laughed, scrambling to his feet. "Rotten shot!"

"More's the pity," yelled Lulu, running over.

"No it wasn't, Lulu," laughed Lennie, "If you'd hit him, your throw wouldn't have gone as far as it did!"

Only then did Bazza realise that Trev was placing the last marker on a spot way beyond his own.

"And the Angels FC long throw-in specialist is – Lulu!"

Bazza had annoyed her so much that her final murderous throw-in had won the competition!

"I think you owe me five pounds," smiled Lulu, holding her hand out beneath his nose.

What a disaster! He'd lost his Twister
Thompson winnings already!

⚽   ⚽

That evening, Bazza sat and brooded.
Bets were good if you won. Losing a bet,
though, was horrible. And losing a bet
to a girl with pigtails was just about as
horrible as it could get.

So, either he'd have to stop betting – or
make sure he won next time. Bazza made
his decision with a grim determination.
He was going to win next time. And to
repair his injured pride, next time simply
had to be a bet to recover his five pounds
from Lulu Squibb.

It was just a case of
working out how to
get her to walk
into another,
superior, trap…

3

Injury Time

When Bazza arrived at school on
Wednesday morning, Twister Thompson
was standing glumly by the gates, a
crisp five pound note between his fingers.

"Make the most of it," scowled Twister,
handing the money to Bazza, "because
you won't be keeping it for long."

"You never spoke a truer word,
Twister!" said Lulu, plucking the note
straight from Bazza's fingers. "A pleasure
to do business with you, Bazza!"

"You – you didn't lose a bet to *her*?" asked Twister as Lulu skipped away with the money.

Bazza nodded glumly. "She won't have it long. I'm going to win it back."

"How?" asked Twister.

"Er...I haven't worked that out, yet."

Twister looked thoughtful. Wickedly thoughtful. "Now I might just be able to help you there," he said slowly.

"Oh, yeah?" Bazza wasn't sure he could trust Twister Thompson any further than he could throw him, with or without a bad arm. But if it helped recover that money it would be worth the risk. "How?"

"By talking her into having another bet. When you win that five pounds back you can give it to me for helping. Then I won't have lost any money."

And I'll have shown Lulu Squibb who's got the superior talent, thought Bazza. He drew Twister to one side so that they couldn't be overheard.

"So what's your idea? It had better be good. I thought I was going to win my bet with her last time!"

Twister gave a little chuckle. "Ah, but last time you didn't have me to help you, Bazza. The bet I'm thinking about now is a sure-fire certainty!"

"A certainty, eh?" Bazza had to hear more about that. "What is it?"

"You bet Lulu Squibb that I'll score a goal next Saturday."

It didn't sound like a certainty to Bazza. "Who are Maddox Rebels playing?" he asked.

"Maddox Rebels," said Twister carefully, "are playing Totton Tykes."

Now that *was* a certainty! "We beat Totton Tykes 12–0!" cried Bazza. "We all banged in a goal! Well, everybody except Tarlock, and he only missed out because he didn't want to score."

"Why not?"

"That's another story,"[2] said Bazza. "The point is, you're bound to score a goal if you're playing Totton Tykes."

Even as he said it, Bazza saw the huge flaw in the plan. "But Lulu will think just the same, won't she? So why would she be

[2] See *Dazzling Dribbling!*

32

daft enough to bet me that you won't score?"

Twister tapped the side of his nose and winked. "Because I'll pretend to be injured. She'll think I'm not even playing!"

"Pretend to be injured? Forget it!" Bazza started to walk away. "That's the trick I worked on her before. She won't fall for it again!"

"Oh yes she will," said Twister, hurrying to his side. "'Cos she's going to see me get injured with her very own eyes…"

The trap was set for next day, at going-home time. Racing out quickly, Bazza and Twister waited near the bike sheds until they saw Lulu coming their way. Then, dropping a tennis ball on to the ground, Twister began dribbling it around.

"Come on then, Wattso," he shouted loud enough for Lulu to hear. "You can't be lucky all the time. Let's see you take the ball off me now!"

Seeing Lulu look their way, Bazza cried, "No problem, Twister! The bike sheds are the goal. If you can score, I'm a baby baboon!"

Dribbling the tennis ball close, Twister hissed, "Right, she's seen us. Time for phase two!"

"Phase two it is," Bazza hissed back. "Go for it."

Shimmying and turning, Twister began racing towards the bike sheds. In front of him, Bazza ran backwards as though waiting for his moment to tackle.

The plan was that Twister wouldn't try to go past him until they were within touching distance of the bike sheds. Then Bazza would pretend to tackle him, after which Twister would pretend to go flying into the bikes and come out pretending to have hurt his leg.

So the last thing Bazza expected was for Twister to forget his own plan and barge into him while there was still a good couple of metres to go. Thrown off balance, Bazza clattered backwards into a mountain bike while, with a graceful dive, Twister dropped carefully to the ground.

"Ooooohhhhhh!" groaned Bazza.

"Aaaagggghhhh!" yelled Twister.

By the time Bazza had pulled himself free and Twister was back on his feet, Lulu had arrived on the scene. "Are you two all right?" she asked.

Twister made a face. "Not sure," he winced. "I think I may have hurt my ankle. I'll have to see how it is tomorrow."

"What about you?" Lulu asked Bazza as Twister limped away.

"You're not going to believe this," said Bazza, gritting his teeth. "I've hurt my wrist!"

Lulu turned on her heel. "You're absolutely right, Bazza. I'm *not* going to believe it!"

Bazza tucked his hand inside his jacket to try to ease the pain. Lulu believing *him* didn't matter so much. The really important question was: would she believe *Twister*?

4

You Twister!

"What do you reckon?" Twister asked Bazza next morning. They were behind the bike sheds again, waiting for Lulu to arrive.

Bazza looked Twister up and down. He'd done a convincing job, there was no doubt about that. Not only had he limped in on a pair of crutches wearing an outsized trainer on his right foot, but somehow he'd managed to change his ankle into one shaped more like a melon.

"How did you get it to look like that?" asked Bazza.

"Four pairs of socks," said Twister, "and a couple of lumps of bath sponge. The trainer belongs to me big brother – and the crutches were in the cupboard under the stairs from when me dad stuck a garden fork through his foot while he was digging the garden!"

"Well it would have fooled me. But will it fool Lulu?"

Twister glanced out towards the front gate. "We'll soon find out. Here she comes!"

Bazza watched as Twister limped away across the playground looking more like Long John Silver than a wicked winger.

He saw Twister nod at Lulu.

He saw Lulu gape at him open-mouthed, point at his ankle, and exchange a few words.

Then, the moment she headed off into school, Bazza raced round the back way and in through a side entrance so that he couldn't help bumping into her as she walked down the corridor towards him.

"Morning, Lulu!" he said brightly.

Lulu didn't waste words. "Have you seen Twister Thompson?"

"No. Why, still sulking after that pitiful attempt to dribble round me with his tennis ball, is he?"

"No, he's—"

Bazza quickly interrupted her. "Looking chirpy? I'm not surprised. He must be relieved he's not facing me again. He knows he'll probably bang in a couple of goals this week."

"No he won't," said Lulu, starting to go pink.

"Lulu, Lulu," said Bazza, shaking his head as though he was talking to a twit. "Face facts. I am a star. He'll never score against me. But against anybody else he's bound to get at least one."

Lulu clenched her fists and tried once more. "Listen, you big banana, I'm telling you Twister Thompson won't score a goal this weekend because—"

"Because you know nothing about marking wickedly tricky wingers!" said Bazza, encouraged by how annoyed Lulu had already become. "Unlike me, the best defender in Defender-land, who knows everything there is to know about wickedly tricky wingers. And I bet you that Twister Thompson *does* score a goal tomorrow!"

It was the last straw. "Right," snarled Lulu, "how much?"

"Five pounds," replied Bazza instantly.

"Done!" said Lulu. "I bet you he *won't* score tomorrow." She grabbed Bazza's hand and shook it to confirm the bet.

"Ouch!" squawked Bazza, wincing as a sharp jab of pain shot up his wrist.

"And stop pretending you've hurt your wrist," snapped Lulu. "Go and have a look at Twister's ankle. That's a real injury!"

Bazza put on his best astonished look. "Twister? Injured ankle?"

"Twister's twisted it!" crowed Lulu. "He was hobbling on crutches when I saw him. So there you go, Mr Big Banana Know-It-All. Even a super whizz-bang tip-top star like you can't score a goal if you're not playing. And by the look of that ankle, Twister won't be playing tomorrow!"

"It worked a treat!" laughed Bazza when he met Twister after school. "She fell for it completely!"

Twister smiled. "So she's bet you that I won't score a goal tomorrow, and you've bet her I will. Right?"

"Right!" grinned Bazza. "And with Maddox Rebels playing against Totton Tykes' leaky old defence you can't fail to score at least one – and I can't lose!"

Twister's smile took a wicked twist. "Maddox Rebels? Oh, silly me. I clean forgot to tell you. I'm not playing for them any more."

"Wha– wha–" burbled Bazza. "Wha– what do you mean?"

"I mean, Bazza the Bighead," said Twister triumphantly, "I've signed on with another team. Welby Wolves!"

"Welby Wolves? But – the Angels are playing Welby Wolves tomorrow! So – I'll be marking you again."

"Yeah," said Twister, frowning. "I was hoping to injure a bit more than your arm when we played our tackling trick on little Squibbo. I was hoping to put you out of the game. Still it doesn't matter now. Having you up against me will make it that much more fun."

"No it won't," snarled Bazza. "An injured arm won't stop me marking you out of the game."

Twister slung his crutches over his shoulder and gave a little dance of joy.

"Ah, but you can't do that, can you? 'Cos if you don't let me score in the game tomorrow…"

Bazza closed his eyes in despair. "I'll lose my bet," he groaned.

5

The Gambler's Last Throw

Bazza was well and truly trapped. If he didn't want to lose his bet, he'd have to risk the Angels losing the match by going easy on Twister and allowing him to score a goal. But if he did that, Lulu would be gunning for him – as she quickly made clear as the teams ran out.

"It's Twister!" cried Lulu, seeing the winger sprint across the pitch in his new colours. "He's playing! For Welby Wolves!"

"Yeah," said Bazza gloomily. "Looks like he made a miracle recovery."

Lulu eyed him suspiciously. "Well just make sure there isn't another miracle, and he scores a goal against the best defender in Defender-land."

"He might," said Bazza. "These things happen."

Standing on tiptoe, Lulu put her fist against Bazza's nose. "He'd better not," she said menacingly. "Because if you let him score to make me lose that bet, then the next thing you'll find happening will be me cleaning my football boots on your shorts – while you're still wearing them!"

And so, not daring to do otherwise, Bazza played his usual game and hardly gave Twister a kick throughout the whole of the first half.

"Silly," hissed the winger as the whistle blew for the half-time break with the score at 0–0. "Very silly. You won't win the money that way. Still, let's hope you see sense in the second half."

"Very good, Bazza," hissed Lulu, "let's hope you see sense in the second half as well."

Bazza's heart fell. Should he resign himself to losing the bet? Or should he give Twister a goal on a plate and resign himself to being chewed into bits by Lulu the Lioness? Was there any way out of this mess? If there was, Bazza couldn't see it.

Glumly he listened to Trev giving his half-time pep talk.

"Their defence are playing well," the Angels coach was saying. "So we're going to have to try to do something from set pieces – free kicks, corners – and don't forget our long throw-in tactic. Bazza, if we get one near their penalty area you move up to join the attack. See if you can get on the end of one of Lulu's long throws. Got that?"

Bazza nodded furiously. He'd got it, all right. It was the perfect excuse. He couldn't be in two places at once. So he'd join the attack at every opportunity. If he could score a few goals himself, then it wouldn't matter if the Wolves got one as a consolation. And if it just happened to be Twister who scored because Bazza wasn't marking him…well, it wouldn't be his fault, would it? Lulu would have to accept that he'd only been obeying Trev's orders!

With renewed hope, Bazza launched himself forward as soon as the match restarted. Charging between two Wolves defenders he screamed for a pass. Mick Ryall played it through as Bazza surged towards the

penalty box – only to find himself beaten
to it by the Wolves goalkeeper kicking it
into touch.

"Lulu! Up you go, Throw-in Champ!"
yelled Lennie Gould.

Lulu sprinted forward to take the throw,
while Bazza ran into the goal mouth to
join the cluster of Angels players waiting
for the ball to arrive.

Except that – it didn't. Even though
Lulu ran in and heaved with all her might,
her throw carried no further than the edge
of the goal area and was easily cleared.

The same thing happened ten minutes later, and again not long after that. Lulu seemed to have completely lost her throw-in power. They were causing no danger at all.

With five minutes left and the score still 0–0, the Angels won yet another throw. Bazza knew it was his last chance. If Twister was going to have time to hit a consolation goal, the Angels had got to score a couple themselves – and pretty soon.

Dashing across to the touchline, Bazza snatched up the ball.

"Hey! I take the throws!" said Lulu, scuttling up.

"Not this one, you don't," said Bazza, taking a couple of steps back. In he ran, pulled his arms back over his head, yanked them forward again – and yelled!

"Owwwww!!"

In the heat of the moment he'd forgotten about his injured wrist. As the pain shot up his arm he dropped the ball – straight at the feet of a Wolves defender, who switched it quickly up the line to Twister Thompson!

"Go, Twister!" screamed the Wolves players.

It seemed as if he must score. With most of the Angels defenders up with the attack, he had a clear run on goal. But, as Kirsten Browne edged out to meet him, a sudden, whirling, screeching Angels-shirted blur caught him up and hammered the ball into touch. Lulu!

"You big cheating banana!" she snarled at Bazza as he struggled back. "You threw that to him on purpose! You wait till the game's over! I'm going to—"

She didn't finish. The throw had been taken, Tarlock Bhasin had won the ball, slid it through to Rhoda O'Neill, and the Angels were on the attack again. With a surging run, Rhoda was closing in on the Wolves goal when she too was stopped by a good tackle and the ball put out for another Angels throw.

"Mine!" roared Lulu, defying Bazza to argue.

Bazza didn't. Knowing that time had almost run out, he trudged forward yet again. There was no hope now. He'd lost the bet. At least if he helped Angels win the match it might make him feel a bit better about things.

The Wolves captain saw him coming. "Twister!" he yelled, pointing at Bazza. "Mark him!"

What a disaster! Instead of him helping Twister score, the game was going to end with Twister trying to stop Bazza!

Or was it? As the Wolves winger tailed him into the goal area, Bazza had an idea. Could it work?

He glanced out to the touchline. It could if Lulu managed to produce a throw-in like she had in the competition. So far today, though, she'd come nowhere near it. Why not?

Because she wasn't annoyed enough, of course! On Tuesday night he'd got her so wound up she could have thrown *him* into the penalty area! But was her temper rising now?

She certainly wasn't calm, that was for sure. As she got ready to take her throw-in,

Bazza could see from the look on her face that she was still steamed up at what she thought was his attempt at cheating.

So…maybe if he irritated her just a little bit more…

"Lulu!" bawled Bazza. "Try and get it past the end of your nose this time, eh?"

From out on the touchline Lulu glared daggers at him. "WHAT?!"

"You heard! Try harder! A worm with a walking stick could manage a longer throw-in than you!"

Even as he said it, Bazza edged back towards the Wolves goal. From right behind him came the voice of Twister Thompson. "She's not happy with you, Bazza. Not happy at all."

He was right. Lulu was steaming up to take the throw as if she was about to burst! "Yaaaaaahhhhhh!!!" she howled, firing the ball straight at Bazza's head just as she had in the competition.

Perfect! Waiting until the rocketing ball was almost on him, Bazza suddenly dived out of the way – so that it smacked the astonished Twister on the head and shot into the roof of the Wolves net for an own goal!

"Yes!" screamed Bazza. "You've scored, Twister! Angels win the match – and I win the bet!!"

After the whistle had gone to give the Angels a 1–0 win, Bazza lost no time in seeking out Lulu in the changing rooms.

She'd seen him coming and had produced the five pound note before he could say a word. "All right, I know what you want. Here it is."

Bazza shook his head. "No, that's not what I want, Lulu. I want to say sorry. Twister nearly made a fool of both of us, and it was all my fault. You keep the money."

"Not likely," said Lulu, breaking into the most enormous grin. "It was worth a fiver just to see my throw hit Twister on the bonce!"

"Let's share it then."

Lulu thrust the money into Bazza's fingers. "No. You have it. You won the bet."

"A bet?" said Trev, coming between them. His voice was icy. "Bazza, do I have to remind you of the Angels code? 'Angels on and off the pitch!' And you can take it from me that angels do not bet!"

Bazza nodded. "I know, Trev. And don't worry, I've learnt my lesson. I've given it up."

"Are you sure, Bazza?"

"Positive, Trev. I'll never bet again!"

"That's easier said than done," said Trev. "I think you will do it again."

"I won't!" cried Bazza, annoyed.

Trev shook his head seriously. He sucked his teeth. "I bet you do," he said solemnly.

"I bet you five pounds I don't!" shouted Bazza.

Even as Bazza realised what he'd said, Trev was whipping the five pound note from his fingers.

"I win!" said Trev. "And let that be a lesson to you, Bazza. Betting's a mug's game."

"What are you going to spend your winnings on, Trev?" laughed Lulu.

"I'm going to put it into club funds," said Trev. "That way it won't be wasted – you can bet on that!"